The Legend of the Lady's Slipper

By Kathy-jo Wargin

Illustrated by Gijsbert van Frankenhuyzen

Sleeping Bear Press

Sleeping Bear Press™

315 E. Eisenhower Parkway, Suite 200
Ann Arbor, MI 48108
www.sleepingbearpress.com

Printed and bound in the United States.

10 9 8 7 6 5 (case)
10 9 8 7 6 5 4 3 2 1 (pbk)

Library of Congress Cataloging-in-Publication Data
Wargin, Kathy-jo.
The legend of the lady's slipper / by Kathy-jo Wargin;
illustrated by Gijsbert van Frankenhuyzen.
p. cm.
Summary: One winter, when the people of her village become
terribly ill, Running Flower braves the snow and freezing cold to
race to the village on the other side of the forest for medicine.
ISBN 978-1-886947-74-0 (case) — ISBN 978-1-58536-168-7 (pbk)
1. Indians of North America—Juvenile fiction.
[1. Indians of North America—Fiction.]
I. Frankenhuyzen Gijsbert van, ill. II. Title.

PZ7.W234 Le 2001
[E]—dc21   2001020718

About the Legend of the Lady's Slipper

A legend is a piece of folklore, which means it is a story that belongs to everyone. Each time a story such as this is retold by a different storyteller, it becomes a unique version of folklore belonging to that individual person.

I heard the legend of the lady's slipper, which is sometimes called the "moccasin flower," many times as a young girl growing up in northern Minnesota. I recall the first time I heard it—I was 8 or 9 years old—and sitting beside a glowing campfire at the edge of a small northern lake. The forest nearby was filled with lady's slippers, and I knew that they were delicate and beautiful creations. Each flower seemed to be handmade by Mother Nature herself.

Although this story has several variations, it is believed that the Ojibwe people of the northern Great Lakes region were the first to tell it. I hope you enjoy my telling of the legend, and enjoy retelling it someday in your own words. But most of all, I hope this story makes you smile.

Kathy-jo Wargin

*This story is dedicated to all young
people and the families they love.*

Showy Lady's Slipper—*Cypripedium reginae*

Long ago, in a lush forest of green and gold, there was a small village. In the center of the village was one large fire with heavy kettles hanging above it, and nearby were several houses made of wood and bark. It was a village of peace, and its people lived a beautiful and simple way of life.

Every night, the children of this village would gather around the fire and warm their faces by the light of the dancing flames.

They would listen to their elders tell magical stories about Amik the beaver, Waboos the rabbit, and Makwa the bear.

As the storytellers spoke, they waved their hands, weaving visions and dreams into tales. At the circle, there was one young maiden who always listened more carefully than the rest. Her name was Running Flower, and she was as swift as the ancient white deer, and more beautiful than the full night sun.

Running Flower lived
with her father, Chief
Spinning Feather, and her
mother, Woman of
Morning Light.

Running Flower admired her mother
greatly, because she taught her to believe
that a brilliant spring always follows the
hardest of winters.

She taught her to honor the frozen ground because beneath the heavy snow, Mother Earth is preparing to grow and live once more.

And this made Running Flower smile.

Running Flower had great respect for her father because he was tall and straight and strong. Sometimes Chief Spinning Feather wore a wide leather band around his head with two eagle feathers dangling from it. She liked how they would spin in the wind when he walked through the forest, and how they would bounce upon his face when he joined in the round dance at night.

Sometimes his face wore a small, steady smile that made her feel very proud.

Running Flower had deep respect for her land and the spirit of her people. She knew she belonged to the woodlands, and in some way, they belonged to her.

And this too, made her smile.

Running Flower shared this love of the forest with everyone in the village. In spring, during the time of the Flower Moon, she would gather forget-me-nots and daisies and place them neatly into the braids of the young girls.

In summer, when it was the Raspberry Moon, she would guide the oldest women deep into the forest, and help them pick sweet red berries to remind them of their youth.

And during the Moon of the Falling Leaves, Running Flower would gather acorns and teach the youngest boys how to spin them like little brown tops.

And this made them smile.

In the deepest part of winter, when only frozen spirits could journey through the land with ease, everyone in the village wore snowshoes to travel through the woods. But not Running Flower. She would dash through the forest wearing nothing on her feet but moccasins.

Many times, when only the pale Winter Moon stood watch, Running Flower would fly upon the paths of the snow-laden woods. She was so swift and light-footed that starlight seemed to fall at her heels.

And this made her smile the most beautiful smile.

One winter, during the time of the Frozen Spirit Moon, the sky brought forth more snow than the people had ever seen. The air was brittle and clear, and a glaze of crystals covered the village. Running Flower noticed that the elders of her village were growing sick. They were coughing and moaning. They were tired and sore.

The sickness grew worse every day, and soon there were no storytellers sitting by the fire at night. During the day, no young braves went to hunt, and there were no kettles hanging over the fire. The smallest children stayed in the lodges, where their mothers kept them warm beneath robes of deer and bearskin.

Even the medicine man was too ill to help. At night, a few young men beat the drum in a loud, impatient way, warning others of their pain.

One evening, Running Flower went to her father. As she stepped into her lodge, she noticed that her mother lay ill by the fire. Her face was warm and moist. Running Flower was very worried, and then she saw that even her father, the great Chief Spinning Feather, was strong no more. His eagle feathers were lying on the ground and his eyes looked old and sad.

Running Flower stepped out of the lodge and put the flat of her hand to her lips and then lifted it generously to the sky.

All at once, she knew what she must do. She knew she had to race to the village on the other side of the forest to find medicine for her people. In the quiet of the night, she donned her white robe and wrapped it tightly around her body. She took her father's eagle feathers from the floor and held them tightly in her hand, and fled into the forest.

Running Flower ran swift like the deer, pressing lightly upon the crust of the moon-showered snow. In the distance she heard the drums of her village pounding through the air. As the wild rhythm raced through her body, she ran along the frozen trails following the light of the polar star.

Running Flower flew with such great speed that her heart began to pulse like a mad-rushing river. She made her way through the thickest areas of forest as the cold night wind raced against her. As she ran, frozen pine needles poked at her face and ice-laden branches lashed at her back.

But all the way, she held her father's feathers tightly in her hand, and they made her strong.

And this made her smile a very brave smile.

Finally, in the time between night and morning, Running Flower reached the distant village. She raised her hand and held her father's feathers up to the face of their chief. He knew then why she came, so he gave her a special pouch from the medicine man. It was small and round, and made from the fur of the fox. There were tails and beads upon it, and it made a beautiful noise as Running Flower slipped back into the forest and raced towards home.

As she ran upon the trail, the soft morning light cast shadows of blue and gray around her, and her body grew feverish. Her face became hot and damp as she struggled against the snow. Running Flower grew too tired and sore to notice the wind and the cold. She no longer felt the sting of the pine needles or the ice upon her feet.

Many times she stumbled, and many times she stopped to rest beneath the shelter of the cedar and spruce trees.

But Running Flower still smiled.

As she neared her village, she heard the beat of the drums once again. The sound made her head pound and her body ache even more. But the brave little girl kept running. She ran until her mind felt as if it were filled with clouds. She ran until her body felt heavy and slow. She ran until she could run no more.

Running Flower let out a terrible wail and fell to the ground.

Two young braves in the village heard her cries and stepped into the forest to find her.

When they did, they saw Running Flower lying in the snow, medicine pouch in one hand, and the feathers of the great chief in the other.

The braves carried her cold, limp body into the village and laid her on a bed of moss. The drums stopped beating and the air was quiet.

Everyone came out to see Running Flower as she lay by the fire with her eyes closed and her mouth still and straight.

The great Chief Spinning Feather walked wearily up to his daughter. He took the medicine pouch from her hand and carefully passed it to his people. Then he lovingly stroked her long black hair and looked up toward the sky.

Woman of Morning Light pressed her cheek to Running Flower's heart, and kissed the frozen tears from her face.

And then, as the chief looked upon her form, he noticed the two eagle feathers still clutched in her hand. With tears in his eyes, he whispered to her that she was very brave, and that springtime would come soon.

But Running Flower did not smile.

In desperation to save her, the women of
the village began to take great pieces of fur
and wrap Running Flower's frozen feet.
They sewed brilliant pink beads and
quills upon them, to honor the young
hero and friend they loved so much.

As the women were busy stitching and sewing, Running Flower took one long last breath, and the feathers dropped quietly from her hand.

Chief Spinning Feather began to weep openly, and Woman of Morning Light collapsed on the ground.

The women, the braves, and the children began to cry. The sound of their sorrow was filling the harsh winter air when in a great flash, the sun burst forth into a glorious show of light.

It was so large and warm it melted months of
snow. New buds appeared on the trees and birds
began to sing.

As everyone watched, the beautiful wrappings upon the feet of Running Flower turned into slippers made of magnificent blossoms and the forest path that Running Flower ran upon became a thick carpet of the most marvelous pink and white flowers anyone had ever seen before.

Everyone watched in amazement as these flowers blossomed behind the soul of Running Flower as she made her way through the forest one last time.

And this made everyone smile.

Today, her footsteps remain in the green and gold forests of the north, far beneath the light of the polar star. Each lady's slipper is a gentle reminder of the beauty and courage that lives in each of us, and of the many different ways that we live on in the hearts of those we love.

And somewhere in that forest, Running Flower will smile forever.

Gijsbert van Frankenhuyzen

Gijsbert van Frankenhuyzen is the renowned illustrator of several Legend titles, including *The Legend of the Sleeping Bear*, *The Legend of Mackinac Island*, and *The Legend of the Loon*. His art captures his lifelong connection to nature and wildlife. Born in the Netherlands, Gijsbert studied at the Royal Academy of Arts in Holland and immigrated to the United States in 1976.

Gijsbert has also illustrated former New York Governor Mario Cuomo's first children's book, *The Blue Spruce*, and he created paintings for another legend by first-time children's author Frank Murphy in *The Legend of the Teddy Bear*. In the fall of 2000, he illustrated *L is for Lincoln: An Illinois Alphabet* written by Kathy-jo Wargin. He also worked with the Mackinac State Park Commission on a book that celebrates historic Mill Creek titled *A Place Called Home: Michigan's Mill Creek Story*. His talent for murals can be seen at Fort Mackinac on Mackinac Island.

Gijsbert lives in Bath, Michigan with wife Robbyn and daughters Kelly and Heather.

Gijsbert would like to thank Lyndsay Bendall, a beautiful Running Flower.

Kathy-jo Wargin

Kathy-jo Wargin is the author of several best-selling children's books, including *The Legend of Sleeping Bear*, *The Legend of Mackinac Island*, *The Legend of the Loon*, *M is for Mitten: A Michigan Alphabet*, *L is for Lincoln: An Illinois Alphabet*, and *The Michigan Counting Book*. Her latest addition to the Legend series is *The Legend of the Lady's Slipper*.

Kathy-jo Wargin is also the author of *Michigan, Spirit of the Land* and *The Great Lakes Cottage Book*, both which she created with her husband, photographer Ed Wargin.

She lives in northern Michigan in a beautiful forest where every spring she finds at least a few delicate lady's slippers. And this, she says, makes her smile.